Looking for Sleepy

Maribeth Boelts

ILLUSTRATED BY Bernadette Pons

ALBERT WHITMAN & COMPANY, MORTON GROVE, ILLINOIS

To Jack and all my little friends on Clearview Drive. —*M.B.*

To François and our little Emma. —*B.P.*

Library of Congress Cataloging-in-Publication Data

Boelts, Maribeth, 1964-
Looking for Sleepy / by Maribeth Boelts ; illustrated by Bernadette Pons.
p. cm.
Summary: When Little Bear protests at bedtime because he cannot find
"Sleepy," Papa helps him look in the bath, in his pajamas, and even in his bed.
ISBN 0-8075-0447-5 (hardcover)
[1. Bedtime—Fiction. 2. Bears—Fiction. 3. Fathers and sons—Fiction.]
I. Pons, Bernadette, ill. II. Title.
.PZ7.B6338Lo 2004 [E] 2003018872

The design is by Carol Gildar.

For more information about Albert Whitman & Company,
visit our web site at www.albertwhitman.com.

Little Bear heard the clock chime. "But I can't go to bed, Papa," Little Bear said. "I don't have any Sleepy yet."

"Let me help you find some Sleepy," Papa said. "Sometimes Sleepy hides under toys."

They sorted blocks—first red, yellow, then blue.

"No Sleepy on the rug," Little Bear said.

"Sometimes it's hungry," Papa said.
Little Bear nibbled two graham crackers
and sipped some milk.

"No Sleepy in the kitchen,"
Little Bear said.

"Sometimes it likes a little swim," Papa said.
Four boats circled in Little Bear's soapy sea.

"No Sleepy in the bathtub," Little Bear said.

"Sometimes it wants to be warm and dry,"
Papa said.
Little Bear zipped his fuzzy pajamas and
stepped into his slippers.

"No Sleepy in my pajamas," Little Bear said.

"Sometimes it likes a story," Papa said.
"Or two stories," Little Bear said.
"Perhaps," said Papa.
Papa read one story about a monkey
and another about a red balloon.

"No Sleepy in my stories," Little Bear said.

"Sometimes it likes a cuddle," Papa said.
He scratched Little Bear's ears and gave him
a kiss on the nose.

"No Sleepy in the cuddle," Little Bear said.

"Sometimes it likes to be left alone," Papa said, "so it can make dreams."

Little Bear thought.
"Sometimes it likes Papa to stay a little
longer," Little Bear said.

"Sometimes it does," Papa whispered.